Muffin

by Anne Rooney
and Sean Julian

Evans

First published 2008 by
Evans Brothers Limited
2A Portman Mansions
Chiltern St
London W1U 6NR

British Library Cataloguing in Publication Data

Rooney, Anne
    Muffin. - (Skylarks)
    1. Children's stories
    I. Title
    823.9'2[J]

ISBN-13: HB 978 0 237 53581 0
ISBN-13: PB 978 0 237 53593 3

Printed in China by WKT Co. Ltd

Series Editor: Louise John
Design: Robert Walster
Production: Jenny Mulvanny

Contents

Chapter One

A white egg rolled down the hill. It rolled and rolled until... bump! It hit a rock.

The little bird inside was tumbled and shaken about. He prodded the shell that was pressed close to his face, pecking and poking until his little black beak pushed through it. Soon, the baby bird blinked in the bright sun. He shook his dizzy head.

A big thing on wheels stopped and bent down to look at the pieces of

eggshell. The chick didn't know that the big thing was a girl called Caitlin, and that the wheels were on her scooter. Caitlin saw the baby bird, sitting in the broken shell.

"Hello," she said. "Who are you?"

As she crouched down to look more closely, her face blocked out the sky above him. The baby bird stared up at her with curious, dark eyes but said nothing. Caitlin looked around. There were no other birds that might look after the baby. She carefully scooped up the spiky, black chick and pushed her scooter home to the lighthouse.

In her room, Caitlin emptied her lunchbox onto the floor. Crumbs and crusts fell on the mat. The bird looked at them.

"You don't want those," said Caitlin, and swept them aside with her hand.

The bird thought that maybe he did want them. He was feeling a little empty in the middle. Caitlin stuffed a rolled-up sock into the lunchbox and settled the baby bird on top. But he just couldn't get comfortable.

The bird opened his black beak. He wondered what sort of noise he could make. A small peeping sound came out. They were both surprised.

"Oh, you're hungry!" said Caitlin. She went away for a long time. When

she came back she leaned over the box
and dropped something slippery and
slightly salty into his open beak. The
bird gulped it down and opened his beak
for more. And when he wasn't empty in

the middle any more, he snuggled into the sock and went to sleep.

But not for long. Soon the emptiness came back and he had to cheep some more. Caitlin closed her lunchbox and carried it downstairs to the kitchen.

Caitlin's dad was sitting at the table reading the paper.

"What's in the box, Caitlin?" he asked.

"Muffin," she said.

"Nuffin? Don't say 'nuffin'. It's 'nothing'. And there is something in there or you wouldn't be carrying it so carefully. Let me see."

Caitlin smiled and opened her lunchbox. The chick was a fuzzy ball perched on top of the sock. He opened his beak as wide as it would go.

"Muffin," she said again. "I'm going to call him Muffin."

"Why Muffin?" asked her dad.

"Because it rhymes."

Dad and Caitlin laughed. But Muffin didn't laugh – it didn't make any sense at all to him.

Chapter Two

Muffin grew and grew. He grew from the size of a table-tennis ball to the size of his rolled-up sock. He grew from the size of a rolled-up sock to the size of Caitlin's guinea pig.

He didn't fit in the lunchbox any more. He waddled about the floor of the lighthouse. His black feet had become orange and his beak had grown as fast as his body. It wasn't black any more, either. When he looked at it with one eye closed, he could see coloured stripes.

Caitlin laid Muffin's food on the stone floor of the kitchen – the slithery, silver, salty things that slipped easily down his throat and wriggled against his insides.

And now Muffin slept in the sleeve of an old jumper. It was warm and snug and smelled of the sea. But he always took his sock with him when he crept into the sleeve.

When Muffin was five weeks old, Caitlin took him outside. The sky was bright and the air tasted salty. The breeze ruffled the sleek black and white feathers that had grown in place of his baby fuzz. Muffin felt good. He stood on a rock. It was knobbly and rough under his webbed feet, not like the smooth, flat stone of the lighthouse floor.

Caitlin's dad was standing by the lighthouse door.

"Good girl," he called. "It's time for him to get used to the outside world, now. He needs to return to the wild."

Each day, Caitlin took Muffin outside. Each day, he stayed longer and longer in the sun and the wind. After five days, Caitlin carried him out, holding him close to her chest. He could feel her heart beating against his folded wing. He smelled the old sea smell of her clothes. Caitlin stroked him gently, and kissed Muffin on the head. As she bent over him, a drop of warm salty water dropped onto his beak.

"Goodbye, Muffin," she said and put him on a rock. She stood for a moment, then ran back into the lighthouse and fetched his sock. She put the sock beside him. And it was time for her to go.

Chapter Three

Muffin waited and waited, but Caitlin didn't come back.

After a long time, he waddled off the rock and into a field. He was beginning to feel empty in the middle again. Where could he find his silver, slithery snacks without Caitlin?

As he walked along he looked around him. A rabbit pricked its ears and bounced away lazily. A couple of birds reeled in the sky above him, tracing loops and curves through the air. One shouted at him:

"What are you doing here?" But it didn't wait for an answer.

The rabbit looked at Muffin, then bent its head to eat the grass.

"Perhaps I could eat grass, too," thought Muffin.

It was hard to pull at the grass with his beak. And the grass didn't taste good.

The rabbit laughed. "You can't eat grass," it said. "You're a bird."

"Oh," said Muffin. "So, what do birds eat?"

The rabbit gave him a strange look.

"Don't you know? What kind of bird are you, if you don't know what you eat?"

Muffin didn't know what kind of bird he was. In fact, until that moment, he hadn't known he was a bird at all.

The rabbit sighed.

"Birds eat... well, let me think. Birds eat seeds. And some eat worms. Try those." And the rabbit hopped away.

Muffin watched the birds around him. A partridge pecked at seeds on the ground. Muffin tried to pick up some seeds. But his beak was too big and it

24

took a long time to pick up even one. The seed was hard and it didn't taste of anything much. It was also very small.

A blackbird landed near him. Then suddenly its head went down and it dragged a long, wriggling worm out of the ground.

"How did you do that?" asked Muffin. "Are they tasty?"

"Try one," said the blackbird. It pulled out another and popped it into Muffin's open beak. The worm wriggled and it was difficult to swallow. It was a bit slithery, but not salty enough.

"Thanks," said Muffin. "Not bad."

But not good, either, he thought, and stomped off.

At last he came to the rocky cliff. Two seagulls were squabbling in the air

above him, snatching something from each other and squawking. A long, slithery, silver thing dropped to the ground. Muffin gobbled it up. It was salty and smooth and it slipped straight down.

"'Ere! You ate my fish!" shouted a gull.

"No, he ate *my* fish!" argued the other. And they carried on fighting.

"So, that's what I eat," thought Muffin. "I eat fish!"

Chapter Four

Now that Muffin's tummy was full he wanted to go to sleep. But he couldn't see any sleeves to crawl into. He looked around. The rooks were flying up to their nests high in the trees.

"If I'm a bird, I must have a nest," thought Muffin, and he waddled over to

a tree. But how to get up? He tried
jumping. No. He tried climbing. No. A
skylark landed near him.

"Make a nest on the floor if you can't
climb," she shouted over her shoulder as
she ran to her own nest, hidden in the
long grass.

"Good idea," said Muffin and began to collect twigs, one at a time, and put them in a pile. His nest wasn't very good. It wasn't very comfy, either. He curled his sock on the top, but the sticks still spiked his bottom.

"This nest is rubbish," sighed Muffin, and he strolled away, pretending it wasn't his at all.

The rabbit appeared again.

"I'm not using my burrow at the moment," she said. "You can use it if you like. I prefer to go out at night."

"Thank you," said Muffin, and crawled into the burrow. It was much more snug than a pile of sticks, and it felt safer, too. He spread out his sock and went to sleep.

It was still dark when the rabbit came

back into the burrow and squashed up
next to Muffin. The rabbit was cosy to
lean on. But in the morning she was
rather grumpy.

"You need to find your own burrow tonight," she said. "There's not enough room for both of us. Off you go!"

Muffin came out of the burrow and screwed up his eyes against the bright sun. Far away, the light glittered on the sea.

"I'll head that way," he thought to himself, and set off.

Muffin didn't walk very fast.

"Caw, you're slow! Why don't you just fly?" shouted a passing crow.

"Fly? I can't fly!" said Muffin.

Muffin looked around him. He tried to see what the other birds were doing. Some jumped from branches and flapped their wings. Some stood on the ground and flapped their wings. He tried flapping his wings. They were

rather stubby. It made his shoulders
ache, and he didn't even get off
the ground.

The rabbit hopped over to Muffin
again, yawning.

"Try jumping," she suggested.

Muffin tried jumping. He bent his
knobbly knees and lowered his tummy to
the ground and tried to push off. But he
toppled forwards. His big beak wedged
into the soft ground and his tail stuck
up in the air.

"You're a rubbish bird!" called an
unkind voice from above.

Muffin prised his beak out of the dirt
and growled. The noise surprised him,
but the unfriendly crow soon flew away.

So Muffin climbed slowly up to a small
rocky ledge and walked off the edge. He

just had time to raise his wings before
his tummy hit the floor. Oooooof!
 "Go jump off a cliff!"
shouted the
unkind crow.

Muffin wasn't hurt, but his feelings were.

"Might as well give it a go," he thought. He waddled to the edge of the cliff. The sea glittered far below. Muffin stood poised on the edge. He closed his eyes, held his breath, spread his wings and took a step forward.

He plummeted down…
and down…
like a stone.

Chapter Five

Muffin hit the water with a big belly flop. His tummy hurt, but he barely noticed because the sparkly water that rushed past him was full of the slithery silver snacks that he loved. His big bill was perfect for snatching them out of the sea. And he found 'flying' much

easier underwater than in the sky.

When Muffin had eaten enough, he let the waves carry him to the shore. He waddled up the beach and began the long trek back toward the rabbit's burrow where he had left his sock.

But soon, his feet were sore. Poor Muffin lay down on the ground beside some rocks and longed to be back in the lighthouse with Caitlin.

The unkind crow flew overhead. It looped the loop and dive-bombed Muffin, laughing.

"You fell in the sea. You can't fly. And you ate a fish! Caw, haw, haw. You're a rubbish bird."

"He's right," Muffin said out loud, "I am a rubbish bird. Birds fly; birds eat worms and seeds; birds sleep in a nest. Birds don't swim; birds don't eat fish; birds don't live in burrows. And birds don't growl."

Then suddenly Muffin heard a growl. A fish fell to the floor in front of him – slithery and silver and long. He looked up.

There were two birds – black and white, just like him. And with orange webbed feet and big colourful beaks, just like his.

"What did you say?" mumbled one, through a beakful of fish.

Muffin sighed.

"I said I'm a rubbish bird. I can't even fly. And birds don't eat fish, and birds don't swim and birds don't live in a burrow. And birds don't growl. Usually."

"Puffins do," said the bird beside him.
"And we can teach you to fly."

"Puffins?"

"Yes," said the other bird. "Would you
like a fish?"

"Am I a puffin?" asked Muffin.

"Yep."

"Muffin the puffin!" he exclaimed.
"Because it rhymes!"

So the puffins shared the fish. Then they waddled to the edge of the cliff, past the burrow where Muffin's egg had rolled out, and jumped off.

Three puffins together, diving into the sparkling sea.

If you enjoyed this story, why not read another *Skylarks* book?

The Black Knight
by Mick Gowar and Graham Howells

One dark night, a mysterious stranger visited *The Green Man* inn. He told the tale of a magnificent treasure, which had been buried nearby in the time of King Arthur. This treasure was protected by The Black Knight. The men in the inn wanted the treasure but they were all too afraid to challenge the fearsome knight. Tom, the innkeeper's nephew, had other ideas...

Yasmin's Parcels

by Jill Atkins and Lauren Tobia

Yasmin lives in a tiny house with her mama and papa and six little brothers and sisters. They are poor and hungry and, as the eldest child, Yasmin knows she needs to do something to help.
So, she sets off to find some food. But Yasmin can't find any food and, instead, is given some mysterious parcels.
How can these parcels help her feed her family?

Ghost Mouse
by Karen Wallace and Beccy Blake

When the new owners of Honeycomb
Cottage move in, the mice that live
there are not happy. They like the
cottage just as it is and Melanie and
Hugo have plans to change everything.
But the mice of Honeycomb Cottage are
no ordinary mice. They set out to scare
Melanie and Hugo away. They *are*
ghost mice after all, and isn't that what
ghosts do best?

Tallulah and the Tea Leaves

By Louise John and Vian Oelofsen

It's the school holidays and Tallulah is bored, bored, BORED! That is, until her Great Granny comes to stay. Tallulah doesn't like Great Granny very much. Not very much at all, really! But, when Great Granny reads the tealeaves, things start to change and Tallulah finds herself in one adventure after another. Suddenly she isn't quite so bored anymore!

Skylarks titles include:

Awkward Annie
by Julia Williams and Tim Archbold
HB 9780237533847
PB 9780237534028

Sleeping Beauty
by Louise John and Natascia Ugliano
HB 9780237533861
PB 9780237534042

Detective Derek
by Karen Wallace and Beccy Blake
HB 9780237533885
PB 9780237534066

Hurricane Season
by David Orme and Doreen Lang
HB 9780237533892
PB 9780237534073

Spiggy Red
by Penny Dolan and Cinzia Battistel
HB 9780237533854
PB 9780237534035

London's Burning
by Pauline Francis and Alessandro
Baldanzi
HB 9780237533878
PB 9780237534059

The Black Knight
by Mick Gowar and Graham Howells
HB 9780237535803
PB 9780237535926

Ghost Mouse
by Karen Wallace and Beccy Blake
HB 9780237535827
PB 9780237535940

Yasmin's Parcels
by Jill Atkins and Lauren Tobia
HB 9780237535858
PB 9780237535971

Muffin
by Anne Rooney and Sean Julian
HB 9780237535810
PB 9780237535933

Tallulah and the Tea Leaves
by Louise John and Vian Oelofsen
HB 9780237535841
PB 9780237535964

The Big Purple Wonderbook
by Enid Richemont and Kelly Waldek
HB 9780237535834
PB 9780237535957